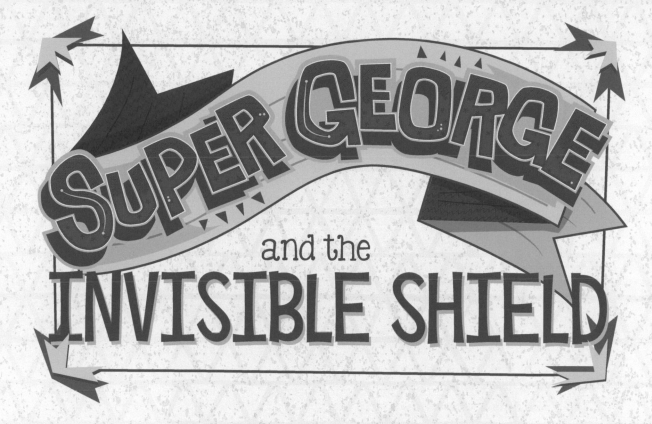

SUPER GEORGE

and the
INVISIBLE SHIELD

SGFPress

Merrimac, Massachusetts

Illustrations in this book were conjured from the artist's imagination using Adobe Photoshop and Adobe Illustrator.

The text type is Amaranth by Gesine Todt & KB Dunk Tank by Khrys Bosland.

Published by SCF Press
P.O. Box 329
Merrimac, Massachusetts 01860

SCFPressMA@gmail.com

For information about ordering bulk copies of this book, please contact the publisher.

ISBN 978-0-9990337-1-5 (paperback)
ISBN 978-0-9990337-0-8 (hardcover)

Library of Congress Control Number: 2017911643

Super George and the Invisible Shield / Mendoza, Laurie P.

1. Teasing–Juvenile Fiction. 2. Mental Health–Juvenile Fiction.
3. Resilience–Juvenile Fiction. 4. Peer relationships–Juvenile Fiction.

2 3 4 5 6 7 8 9 0 1

Second printing 2017

Printed in the United States

Dedication

With love to all my "Georges."
You know who you are.

~ LPM

Dedicated to the imagination
of every kid everywhere.

~ CF

George loved superheroes.

When he was in a crime-fighting mood,
he wore his cape to school.

He liked it when people called him Super George.

The trouble started when people called him other names.

"Hi, Curious George," Leah said.

"DON'T SAY THAT!"

George yelled.

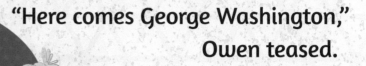
"Here comes George Washington," Owen teased.

"DON'T SAY THAT!"
George yelled.

"Good morning, King George,"
joked the custodian,
Mr. Robertson.

"DON'T SAY THAT!"

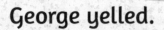
George yelled.

Whenever George yelled, he imagined the sound racing out of his mouth, getting bigger and bigger and bigger until it crashed against the other person like storm waves against a rocky shore, stopping them from saying things he didn't like.

Unfortunately for George, it never worked that way. No matter how much he yelled, people kept making him mad. Worst of all, *he* was the one who kept getting in trouble!

Ms. Takada would say,

"We speak respectfully in Room 26, George. Please sit in the Cool-Down Corner until you're calm enough to rejoin the class."

"THEY STARTED IT!"

he'd shout.

"THEY MADE ME MAD!"

"No one else can make you mad," she'd reply.

"When you let their words upset you, you're letting them steal your power."

Stomping to the Cool-Down Corner, George would yell,

"IT'S NOT FAIR!"

One day after school, George was watching a TV show starring his favorite superhero, Silent Knight.

Silent Knight's arch enemy, Bedlam, was one nasty customer.

"DON'T LET HIM SAY THAT!"

George yelled at the television.

But Silent Knight never tried to stop Bedlam's words.
Instead, he would say,

"My shield is up,
It's blocking you,
Words bounce right off,
They can't break through."

Silent Knight's invisible shield sucked the strength
right out of Bedlam's words, making them harmless.

George was desperate to get one just like it.

While Grandma cooked dinner, George told her about Silent Knight vs. Bedlam.

"I wish I had an invisible shield," he said.

"Maybe you do," Grandma replied.

George shook his head.

"I don't think so. If I do, it's broken."

"It could be like a muscle you never use," Grandma said.
"Remember when I started going to the gym?
  My muscles were flabby and weak.
  Now I exercise every day so
  they're much stronger."

"But how could I make my shield stronger?"
George asked.

Grandma thought for a moment.

"Most muscles need two things:
  oxygen and regular exercise.
  Try taking some deep breaths."

She showed George how to slowly breathe in through his nose...

and blow out through his mouth.

After several breaths he felt calmer,
but he still wasn't convinced.

"If I have a shield, then where's the activation button?" he asked.

"Here?"
Grandma joked,
tickling his belly.

George placed
the tip of his finger
into his belly button and pressed.

He thought he heard a quiet hum followed
by the soft click of something sliding into place.

After dinner and a bath, George jumped into bed.

He breathed deeply, exercising his invisible shield until he fell asleep.

The next morning after breakfast, George put on his cape and zoomed down the block. Two kids were already at the bus stop.

"Hi Super George," Jenna said.

"Hi," George said back.

"Hey, it's Georgie Porgie," Owen laughed.

George opened his mouth.

"DON'T S--"

He stopped. He breathed in through his nose... and blew out through his mouth. When he squinted his eyes, he could almost see Owen's words bouncing off his invisible shield and falling to the ground. He spoke firmly, without yelling.

"Call me George."

Owen shrugged, then turned to talk to Jenna.

The shield had worked! Was it getting stronger?

George tapped Jenna on the shoulder.

"Say something mean to me."

Jenna looked at him like he was crazy. "What?"

"Say something mean, please."

"For real?" Jenna asked.

George nodded.

"Okay. You're silly," Jenna said with a smile.

"You're not trying," George said.

Jenna stopped smiling. "You're an idiot."

George felt **idiot** ping off his shield. Easy peasy!

"Meaner," he said.

"Get lost Jerky George," Jenna said.

George made sound effects in his head and the words clattered to the sidewalk like a handful of pebbles. He felt his power growing.

"Super mean!" he demanded.

"You look like a loser wearing that cape," Jenna said.

Uh-oh.

George's jaw muscles tightened.

He felt a yell rising inside his chest.

He jabbed at his belly button trying

to activate his shield. It wasn't working!

Holy Meltdown, Super George!

With no time to spare, George took one deep breath
and then another to give his shield oxygen.

It gave him a moment to think.

My shield is up,
It's blocking you,
Words bounce right off,
They can't break through.

Jenna was still looking at him.
"I said, you look like a loser wearing that cape,"
she repeated.

"I don't care what you say,
I like wearing it," George replied.

Thud.

Thud.

Thud.

Jenna's words dropped to earth like a bucket of bricks.
"You definitely have your own style," she said.

George's muscles relaxed. The yell shrank like a deflating balloon.

The bus rumbled up and George boarded.
He could tell his shield was stronger already.

"Hi Curious George," Leah said.

Pew, Pew, Pew!

George felt confident his invisible shield was going to help him stay out of the Cool-Down Corner.

"Call me Super George," he said.

He swept his cape to one side and climbed into his seat.

Activate Your Shield

Breathe in through your nose...

My shield is up,
It's blocking you,
Words bounce right off,
They can't break through.

BUS

...and out through your mouth.

CPSIA information can be obtained
at www.ICGtesting.com
Printed in the USA
LVHW07n2310040718
582674LV00011B/270/P